The DINKY

Christine Harder Tangvald

illustrated by Kathleen Estes

STANDARD
PUBLISHING
Cincinnati, Ohio

Text © 1995 by Christine Harder Tangvald. Illustrations © 1995 The Standard Publishing Company, Cincinnati, Ohio. A division of Standex International Corporation. All rights reserved. Printed in the United States of America. Designed by Coleen Davis. ISBN 0-7847-0168-7

"Who ...
whoooo ...
whoooo will
carry Mary?"

asked the
Wise Old Owl.

"All the big donkeys
are working in the fields.
Whoooo will carry Mary?"

"I will,"
said Rinky Dinky
Donkey. "I will
carry Mary."

"Oh, NO!" shouted the other animals in the yard. "You are *Rinky Dinky* Donkey. You can't carry Mary! You are TOO little!"

"I am *not* too little," said Rinky Dinky Donkey. "I am big enough to carry Mary!"

"Yes," said the Wise Old Owl, "I think you CAN do it. But you must be very *very* careful.

"You must not stumble.
You must not fall.
You must not
wobble —
not at ALL!

"Because Mary is going
to have a *baby!*"

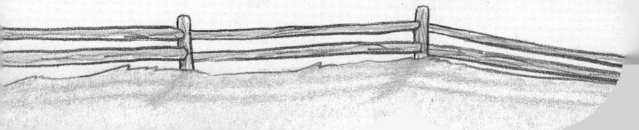

"I will be *very* careful," said Rinky Dinky Donkey. "I will not stumble. I will not fall. I will not w_ob^le — not at ALL!"

Joseph and Mary smiled at Rinky Dinky Donkey. And carefully, Mary climbed up on his back.

Clip-clop, clip-clop.
Up, up, up the steep, steep hills,
Rinky Dinky Donkey
carried Mary.

**Clip-clop,
clip-clop.
Down, down, *down*
the steep, *steep* hills,
Rinky Dinky Donkey
carried Mary.**

Clip-clop, clip-clop.
Rinky Dinky Donkey began to get hot . . .
and *thirsty* . . .
and *tired* . . .
very, *very* tired!

He was *so* glad when Mary and Joseph stopped to rest!

In the cool shade,
after a long drink,
Rinky Dinky
Donkey began
to feel *V-E-R-Y*
sleepy.

"Look at the poor donkey," he heard Mary say. "His ears are drooping! His tail is drooping!

"His *tongue* is drooping! I don't think he can go on!"

"Oh, *dear!*" said Rinky Dinky Donkey. "Maybe I *am* too little to carry Mary after all."

"But the Wise Old Owl said
I am big enough! Yes!
I *am* BIG enough!
I CAN DO IT!"

And slowly,
S-L-O-W-L-Y,
Rinky Dinky
Donkey got up!

**Clip-clop,
clip-clop.**

Up and down and around the hills,

Rinky Dinky Donkey carried Mary
all the way
to Bethlehem!

And late that night,
when the stars
shone bright,
in a little stable
in Bethlehem,

Mary's baby was born!
And that baby was
Jesus —
God's own Son!

"Wow!" whispered Rinky Dinky Donkey as he smiled down at the baby.

"I was *very* careful," he said.
"I did not stumble.
I did not fall.
I did not w$_o$b$_b$l$_e$ —
not at ALL!"